Dear Parent:

Congratulations! Your child is taking the first steps on an exciting journey. The destination? Independent reading!

STEP INTO READING® will help your child get there. The program offers five steps to reading success. Each step includes fun stories and colorful art. There are also Step into Reading Sticker Books, Step into Reading Math Readers, Step into Reading Phonics Readers, Step into Reading Write-In Readers, and Step into Reading Phonics Boxed Sets—a complete literacy program with something to interest every child.

Learning to Read, Step by Step!

Ready to Read   **Preschool–Kindergarten**
• big type and easy words • rhyme and rhythm • picture clues
For children who know the alphabet and are eager to begin reading.

Reading with Help   **Preschool–Grade 1**
• basic vocabulary • short sentences • simple stories
For children who recognize familiar words and sound out new words with help.

Reading on Your Own   **Grades 1–3**
• engaging characters • easy-to-follow plots • popular topics
For children who are ready to read on their own.

Reading Paragraphs   **Grades 2–3**
• challenging vocabulary • short paragraphs • exciting stories
For newly independent readers who read simple sentences with confidence.

Ready for Chapters   **Grades 2–4**
• chapters • longer paragraphs • full-color art
For children who want to take the plunge into chapter books but still like colorful pictures.

STEP INTO READING® is designed to give every child a successful reading experience. The grade levels are only guides; children can progress through the steps at their own speed, developing confidence in their reading, no matter what the grade.

Remember, a lifetime love of reading starts with a single step!

Three Fairy Tales

Step into Reading, Random House, and the Random House colophon are registered trademarks of Random House, Inc.

Visit us on the Web!
StepIntoReading.com
www.randomhouse.com/kids

Educators and librarians, for a variety of teaching tools, visit us at www.randomhouse.com/teachers

ISBN: 978-0-7364-2812-5

MANUFACTURED IN CHINA   10 9 8 7 6 5 4 3 2

Disney fairies

TinkerBell

Three Fairy Tales

Step 3 Books

A Collection of Three Early Readers

Random House ⌂ New York

Contents

STEP INTO READING®

STEP 3

A Fairy Tale

By Apple Jordan
Illustrated by the Disney Storybook Artists

Random House 🏠 New York

It was a special day

in Pixie Hollow.

All the fairies gathered around.

With a sprinkling of pixie dust,

a new fairy was born.

Her name was Tinker Bell.

Queen Clarion welcomed

the newest fairy.

"Born of laughter.

Clothed in cheer.

Happiness

has brought you here."

The fairies tried to help

Tinker Bell find her talent.

They gave her

flowers, water, and light.

But everything Tink

touched faded away.

Then Tinker Bell
passed a hammer.
It began to glow.
It flew straight toward her.
She had found her talent.
She was a tinker fairy.

The tinker fairies came
to welcome Tinker Bell.
Tink was happy to meet them.
She was also a bit sad.
Tinkers weren't fancy
like the other fairies.

Tink's new friends,
Clank and Bobble,
took her on a tour
of Pixie Hollow.
They saw all the fairies
getting ready for spring.
"It's the changing of the seasons!"
explained Bobble.

There was a lot going on

at Tinkers' Nook.

Tinker Bell loved seeing

all the useful things

the tinker fairies made.

Fairy Mary was the head tinker.
She told Clank and Bobble
to deliver their creations
to the rest of the fairies fast.
They would need the items
on the mainland.
"The mainland sounds
flitterific!" cried Tink.

The tinker fairies
showed the queen
what they had made.
One of Tinker Bell's creations
still needed some work.
Tink would fix it in time
to take it with her
to the mainland.

The queen told Tink that
tinker fairies did not go
to the mainland.
"Your work is here
in Pixie Hollow,"
Queen Clarion said.

"Being a tinker stinks,"
said Tinker Bell
back at Tinkers' Nook.
Fairy Mary told her that
she should be proud
of who she was.

But Tinker Bell did not

want to be a tinker.

She wanted to be a nature fairy.

She asked her friends

for help.

First Silvermist
tried to teach Tink
how to be a water fairy.
But Tink was not good
with water.

Then Iridessa tried to teach

Tink how to be a light fairy.

But Tink was not good

with light.

Fawn tried to show Tink
how to be an animal fairy.
But Tink was not good
with animals, either.

Tink saw a
big bird flying in the sky.
"Maybe that guy can help,"
she said.
The bird made a
nosedive for Tink.
"Hawk!" yelled the fairies
as they ran for cover.

Tink jumped into a hole to hide.

The hole was Vidia's hiding spot.

Now the hawk

was after Vidia, too.

The other fairies

attacked the hawk with berries.

Vidia was safe.

But she was angry.

Tink tried to help her clean up,

but she didn't want Tink's help.

Tink felt horrible.

She couldn't hold drops of water.

She couldn't hold rays of light.

Baby birds were afraid of her.

"I'm useless," she said.

Tink flew to the beach.

She wanted to be alone.

There she spotted

a broken music box.

Tink quickly got to work.

Her friends watched.

"You fixed it!" Silvermist cried.

They were all amazed

at her tinkering talent.

Tinker Bell enjoyed tinkering.

But she still wanted to go

to the mainland.

As her last hope,

Tink went to Vidia for help.

But Vidia was still angry

with her.

Vidia got an evil idea.

She said Tink should capture

the Sprinting Thistles

to prove she was a garden fairy.

It was a dangerous job.

But Tink had to try.

It was her last chance.

She made a corral and a lasso

to capture the Thistles.

She saddled up

Cheese the mouse and

was on her way.

"It's working!" cried Tink.

Thistles went into the corral!

But then Vidia blew

a strong gust of wind.

The corral gate flew open.

The Thistles ran out.

Hundreds of other Thistles
ran by, too.
Tinker Bell lost control of them.
The Thistles ran this way
and that way through
Springtime Square.
They destroyed all
the springtime supplies.

Everyone was upset.

Spring would have to be canceled.

It was all Tinker Bell's fault.

She flew away in shame.

Tinker Bell decided to leave
Pixie Hollow for good.
She stopped one last time
at the tinkers' workshop.
As she looked around,
she got an idea.
She knew how to save spring!

Back at Springtime Square,
Vidia was punished for
helping the Thistles escape.
And everyone was sad that
spring wouldn't be coming.
"Wait!" Tinker Bell cried.
"I know how we can
fix everything!
But I can't do it alone."

The fairies were eager to help.
Tink showed everyone
what to do.
In the blink of an eye,
Tink's creations filled buckets
with berry paint and seeds.
Soon everything
was ready for spring.

"You did it!"
exclaimed Queen Clarion.
"You saved spring!"
"We *all* did it,"
said Tinker Bell.

Fairy Mary told Tink
she could go to
the mainland, too.
The music box Tink had fixed
belonged to a special little girl.
And only Tinker Bell could
deliver it to her.

Tinker Bell was happy.

Her tinkerings had saved spring.

She was a tinker fairy—

and proud of it!

Tink's Treasure Hunt

By Melissa Lagonegro

Illustrated by Denise Shimabukuro, Jeff Clark,
Merry Clingen, Adrienne Brown, Charles Pickens,
and the Disney Storybook Artists

Random House 🏠 New York

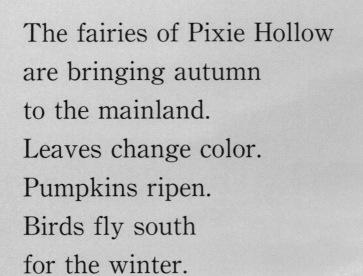

The fairies of Pixie Hollow
are bringing autumn
to the mainland.
Leaves change color.
Pumpkins ripen.
Birds fly south
for the winter.

In Pixie Hollow,
the dust-keeper fairies pack
and deliver pixie dust.
Fairies need pixie dust
to fly and to make magic.

After work,
Terence visits Tinker Bell.
She is building a boat.

Tink takes her boat for a ride.
She speeds through the water.
"Oh, no!" she cries.
Her boat crashes!
Luckily, she isn't hurt.

Then Queen Clarion
calls Tink to her chamber.
The Minister of Autumn is there.

He tells Queen Clarion,
Fairy Mary, and Tink
about the Autumn Revelry.

Every year, the fairies create
a special autumn scepter.
This year, it's Tink's turn
to make it!

She must build the scepter
with a very rare moonstone.
The blue harvest moon's rays
will pass through the moonstone.
It will create blue pixie dust
for the Pixie Dust Tree!

Terence helps Tink.

Tink molds metal.

Terence keeps the fire burning.

The two fairies make a great team.

They work together
day and night.
Tink sets the moonstone.
It is very heavy.
Terence gives Tink advice.

"Steady," he says.
Tink gets annoyed.
A piece breaks off the setting.
Terence goes to find
a tool to fix it.

Finally, Tink finishes
the scepter.
Terence returns with a compass.
He thinks its parts
will fix the broken setting.
But Tink is still annoyed.
She pushes the compass
out of the way.

The compass rolls
into the scepter.
The scepter breaks into pieces!
Tink is angry with Terence.

Tink tells Terence to leave.
Then she kicks the compass.
It smashes into the moonstone!
Tink is very upset.

Clank and Bobble visit Tink.
They invite her to
the Fairy-Tale Theater.
She agrees to go.

The show is about
the Mirror of Incanta.
The mirror can grant one wish.
But it was lost in a shipwreck
on a faraway island.
Tink wants to find the mirror!
She wants to use the wish.
She wants to fix
the broken moonstone.

Tink draws a map
of the faraway island.
She makes a list.
She gathers supplies
and checks the compass.
She has a plan!

Tink builds a balloon.
She uses cotton balls
and a gourd.
She works very hard.

The balloon is finished.

Tink hops in.

She flies away from Pixie Hollow.

It is late. Tink is hungry.
But her food is gone!
A firefly named Blaze
ate it all.

Blaze shines his light.
Now Tink can read her map.
Blaze can help Tink
on her trip!

Soon Tink finds the island.

She sets out to explore.

Blaze stays with the balloon.

The balloon breaks loose.

Blaze tries to warn Tink.

But it is too late.
Tink's balloon floats away.
Now her supplies are gone!

Tink is hungry.

Blaze calls for his friends.

They bring honey and water.

Then they show Tink the way.

Back in Pixie Hollow,
Terence goes to Tink's house.
He finds moonstone pieces,
the list, and the
balloon drawing.
Tink needs his help!
He goes to find her.

Tink and Blaze sneak
past two trolls.
Tink knows
the mirror
can't be far!

They find the shipwreck!
"This is it!" Tink cries.
She must go inside
to find the mirror
and fix the moonstone.

Tink and Blaze go into
the dark and spooky ship.
Blaze lights the way.

They find the mirror!

"I wish . . . ," Tink begins.

But Blaze buzzes in her ear.

She tries again.

Blaze buzzes some more.

"Blaze, I wish you'd be quiet!"

Tink yells.

Blaze stops buzzing. Oh, no!
Tink used her one wish!
Her eyes fill with tears.
"I wish Terence were here,"
she cries.
Then she sees him
in the mirror.

Terence found Tink.

He is on the ship!

Tink is so happy to see him.

The two friends hug.

Just then,
rats surround them!
Blaze pretends to be a monster.
He makes a big shadow.
The rats are scared.
They run away.
"Let's go," says Terence.

They find the balloon!
Tink has an idea.
She and Terence can fix
the scepter with the
moonstone pieces.
They work together.
Blaze helps.

Back in Pixie Hollow,
the Autumn Revelry begins.
Tink presents the scepter.
The moonstone is in pieces.
But moonbeams reflect
off each piece.
Blue pixie dust rains down.
There is more blue dust
than ever before!

This Autumn Revelry
is the best one ever!
Everyone thanks Tink
and her very special friends.

Disney fairies

TinkerBell
AND THE
GREAT FAIRY RESCUE

Vidia Takes Charge

By Melissa Lagonegro
Illustrated by
the Disney Storybook Artists

Random House 🏠 New York

Tinker Bell and her friends
are bringing summer
to the mainland!

Terence and Tinker Bell fly
to fairy camp.
This is where the fairies
prepare for summer.

One fairy paints lovely lines

on a butterfly's wings.

Other fairies teach crickets to sing.

Everyone is very busy!

Suddenly, humans drive by.

The fairies hide so the humans

cannot see them.

But Tinker Bell is curious.

She follows the humans' car.

Vidia is a fast-flying fairy.

She speeds after Tink

and tries to stop her.

Tink peers at the humans.

They get out of the car.

A little girl named Lizzy skips

into the house.

Her father carries their luggage.

Tink wants to look
at the car.
She flies into the engine.
"Vidia, this is amazing,"
says Tink.
But Vidia is angry.

"You shouldn't be this close!"

she yells.

Tink is too busy to listen.

She pulls a lever.

Water sprays out at Vidia.

Now Vidia is angry and wet.

Soon, the humans come back.

Tink and Vidia quickly hide.

Lizzy and her father

catch a butterfly.

They look at its pretty wings.

Lizzy believes that fairies

painted them.

But her father does not believe
in fairies.
"Fairies are not real,"
he tells Lizzy.

Tink and Vidia try to leave.

But Vidia can't fly.

Her wings are still wet.

Tink tells Vidia she's sorry.

Vidia just yells at Tink.

But Tink isn't listening.
She sees a fairy house
that Lizzy made.
"Wow!" says Tink.

Tink goes into the house.

She starts to explore.

"We're not supposed

to go near human houses!"

warns Vidia.

But Tink won't listen.

Vidia decides to teach

Tink a lesson.

She makes a great gust of wind

slam the door shut.

Now Tink is locked

inside the fairy house!

Lizzy catches Tink.

She puts Tink in a birdcage

so the cat cannot reach her.

Vidia watches from the window.

She did not mean

for Tink to get caught!

Vidia rushes back to fairy camp.

She tells the other fairies that

Tink is trapped.

"We have to hurry and save her!"

cries Vidia.

But a storm has begun.

The fairies cannot fly

in the rain.

Clank and Bobble have an idea.

"We're going to build a boat,"

they tell everyone.

At Lizzy's house,

Tink is scared.

But Lizzy does not want

to hurt Tink.

Lizzy shows Tink
her fairy drawings.
Tink realizes how much
Lizzy loves fairies.

Lizzy's father hears Lizzy
talking to Tink.
He goes to her room.
But Lizzy wants
to keep Tink a secret.
She hides Tink
until her father leaves.

Tinker Bell is ready to leave.

Lizzie wants her to stay.

"There's so much we can do,"

pleads Lizzie.

Tink teaches Lizzy
about fairies.
Lizzy takes notes.
Tink helps Lizzy paste them
in her journal.

Meanwhile,

Vidia and the other fairies

sail to Tink.

Their rescue boat goes

over a waterfall!

Silvermist makes a water slide

to keep the fairies safe.

Soon, Tinker Bell leaves.

She looks in the window

and sees Lizzy.

Lizzy wants to show her father
the fairy journal.
But her father does not
have time for her.
He is too busy fixing leaks.

Tink decides to stay

with Lizzy a little longer.

Lizzy is very happy.

That night,

the rescue team gets

in more trouble!

Vidia is stuck

in the mud.

The other fairies try

to help her.

But a car is coming!

Iridessa makes the driver stop

and get out of the car.

The fairies grab his shoelace.

The shoelace pulls them

out of the mud!

Tink wants to help
Lizzy and her father.
She tinkers with the leak
in their house.
She fixes it!

Tink sees a butterfly
in the office.
Lizzy's father trapped it
in a jar to study it.
Tink decides to set
the butterfly free.

Lizzy's father is very angry

that his butterfly is gone.

He blames Lizzy.

Meanwhile,

Vidia tells the other fairies

that she trapped Tink

in the fairy house.

"This is not your fault,"

says Rosetta.

The fairies vow to work together

to find Tink.

Tink sprinkles Lizzy
with pixie dust
to cheer her up.
Lizzy flies!

The rescue team arrives.

Lizzy's cat corners them.

The fairies distract the cat

while Vidia looks for Tink.

Lizzy's father goes

to Lizzy's room.

Tink flies up to him.

She proves that fairies are real.

Lizzy's father is shocked!

He tries to catch Tink.

Vidia arrives just in time.

She pushes Tink

out of the way.

But Lizzy's father

catches Vidia instead!

Lizzy begs her father
to let Vidia go.
But he refuses.
Now Tink must rescue Vidia!

The other fairies agree to help.
Lizzy wants to help, too.
The fairies sprinkle Lizzy
with pixie dust.
"All aboard!"
Tink tells the fairies.

Lizzy and the fairies

find Lizzy's father.

He can't believe that

Lizzy is flying!

"It has to be magic," he says.

"It is," says Lizzy. "Fairies!"

Lizzy's father believes her.

And he finally believes

in fairies.

He lets Vidia go.

The next day,

the fairies have a tea party

with Lizzy and her father.

Lizzy pours tea.

The fairies bring flowers.

The fairies watch
Lizzy and her father
read together.
Tink smiles.
Her tinkering has fixed a leak
and a family!

Meet the Fairies!

Tinker Bell

Talent: Tinker fairy

Lives in: A teakettle

Hobbies: Inventing things, going on adventures

Personality: Fun-loving, brave

Favorite flower: Silver bell

Favorite food: Pumpkin muffins

148

Terence

Talent: Dust-keeper fairy

Lives in: The dust-keepers' dorm

Best Friend: Tinker Bell

Hobbies: Helping his friends, searching for objects for Tinker Bell's inventions

Personality: Kind, caring

Favorite food: Strawberry cake

Vidia

Talent: Fast-flying fairy

Lives in: A sour-plum tree

Hobbies: Racing dragonflies, flying alone

Personality: Cool, proud

Favorite flower: Prickly pear blossom

Favorite food: Lemon tarts

Rosetta

Talent: Garden fairy

Lives in: A rose

Hobbies: Giving makeovers, dressing up

Personality: Sweet, sassy

Favorite flower: Rose

Favorite food: Buttercup soup

Silvermist

Talent: Water fairy

Lives: Near the babbling brook

Hobbies: Training tadpoles, making dewdrops

Personality: Warm, loving

Favorite color: Blue

Favorite flower: Water lily

Iridessa

Talent: Light fairy

Lives in: A sunflower

Hobbies: Training fireflies

Personality: A leader, cheery

Favorite color: Gold

Favorite food: Lemon pie

Fawn

Talent: Animal fairy

Lives in: A pinecone tree house

Hobbies: Playing leapfrog and fairy tag

Personality: Sporty, fun

Favorite flower: Tiger lily

Favorite food: Acorn butter